D1307747

The Elegant Cockroach

Love, Longing & Six Legs

WRITTEN
by

DEIDRE ANNE MARTIN

ILLUSTRATED
by

STEFANIE AUGUSTINE

UPPERCASE

CREDITS

Story by Deidre Anne Martin
Illustration by Stefanie Augustine

Design by Janine Vangool
Set in Benton Modern Display

Printed in China by Everbest Printing
© 2010

UPPERCASE

204, 100 - 7th Avenue SW
Calgary, Alberta, Canada T2P 0W4

www.uppercasegallery.ca
www.uppercasemagazine.com
shop.uppercasegallery.ca

ISBN 978-0-9866502-1-5

He was no Apollo, but the Elegant Cockroach had something.

Strange, sad charm
set him apart.

His eyes were clear blue
and deep-set and
he had a sharp nose,
giving his face an almost
wolfish appearance.

His long lanky limbs
seemed custom-built for
the display of fineries.

He
wore
his
trousers
tight
and
stove-
pipe
skinny.

His movements // were delicate

and he walked
with a gangster's
slouchy grace.

The Elegant
Cockroach
was elegant,

but

style isn't everything.

The Elegant Cockroach lived alone,

quietly.

He had grown tired of excitement.

The jazzy violence of the big city,
the constant moonlighting,
all that glitz and melodrama—
it was simply no longer his cup of tea.

The Elegant Cockroach
had experienced
a change of heart.

More and more, he was becoming
a fan of the old-school. He suffered nostalgia
for the beauty and slowness of earlier times.
In his dreams he lived in the age of
speakeasys and town hall dances.

He tried to keep this age and its
disappearing customs alive by sending
handwritten letters through the post
and using colourful little expressions
in his daily exchanges with others:

People may have
laughed at him
when he said
these things,

That's the
berries!

but he did so anyway,
just to help keep
lightness in the air.

A misfit in the city and among his kind,
he had grown increasingly fond of nature.

Nature is slow and needs
to be taken in that way.
He believed in the
magnificence of trees.

Sometimes he would walk deep
into the woods and longingly observe the
happiness of wild animals.

He wandered around and
wondered silently to himself,

*"how
to find
that?"*

At home in his kitchen, the Elegant Cockroach took joy in the nightly ritual of washing up.

His dwellings were modest but refined. All he had was one bedroom and a small parlor for entertaining.

Wallpaper the colour of aubergines added a touch of decadence that no longer suited his tastes.

These days, the colour made him queasy.

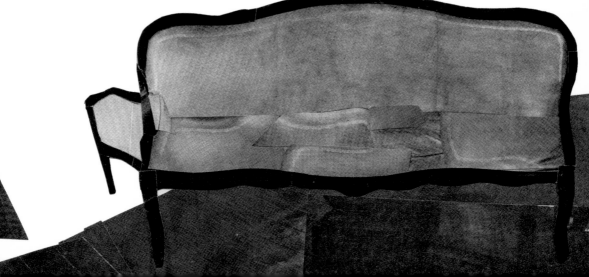

He wished that
he had kept
the walls bare.

No stranger to bad weather,
the Elegant Cockroach sometimes
felt as though life were closing in
on him like a giant umbrella.

He wore
the soles
of his
shoes
down

searching
everywhere,

rain
or shine,

for a place
to belong.

During these tough times,
he put his faith in literature.
This was daring.

Too much could hurt him,
same as nature.

Sometimes his loneliness
was so thick he felt he could slice it
like a loaf of Russian rye bread.

It tasted strong.

To raise his spirits,
the Elegant Cockroach
decided to learn

the Spanish guitar.

Learning through play was
old-school and he liked that.
The instrument he chose
was awfully elegant but there
was nobody around to listen
to his pretty melodies.

Birdsong
outside
his window

made him

happier.

After a long while
the Elegant Cockroach
came to accept the
changes he felt inside

and that he alone
could not make
the difference.

What he needed was

the closeness
of another.

Someone to lean on,
to stand out for him,
warm his feet on a cold night,
hold his hand
when the world spun too fast.

Maybe someday,

he hoped,

a dazzling stranger would cross his path,
stick around awhile...

...share this life.

THE END